Jubilee: "Talk about extra crispy—"

Now, you might ask, *how can a robot hate anything*? Well, the thing is, most Sentinels don't. They were just programmed by this weird scientist who was convinced mutants were a threat to mankind. So their programming told them to find and stomp all mutants.

But the Sentinels in the Ant Hill were different. Their leader had actually started thinking on his own. Professor X uses some special word to describe it—*sentient*, I think—but all I know is, this robot started having his own ideas. Like, *how about building this big machine that will cause a solar flare that would turn all of us humans crispier than chili fries*?

The Xavier Files

by Justine Korman

cover illustration by Dana and Del Thompson

text illustrations by Aristides Ruiz

Bullseye Books

Random House 🏠 New York

A BULLSEYE BOOK PUBLISHED BY RANDOM HOUSE, INC.

Copyright © 1994 by Marvel Entertainment Group, Inc. All rights
reserved under International and Pan-American Copyright Conven-
tions. Published in the United States by Random House, Inc., New
York, and simultaneously in Canada by Random House of Canada
Limited, Toronto. All rights reserved.
Library of Congress Catalog Card Number: 93-73435
ISBN: 0-679-86177-7
RL: 3.9

Manufactured in the United States of America   10 9 8 7 6 5 4 3 2 1

MARVEL COMICS® and X-MEN® are registered trademarks of
Marvel Entertainment Group, Inc.

X-MEN®

The Xavier Files

PROLOGUE
....

The following was recorded by Professor Charles Xavier on the secret hard drive of the Cerebro supercomputer.

---

file: journal
password: Xavier files

For over twenty years now it has been my privilege to lead the original X-Men and subsequent teams of mutants dedicated to protecting humankind. The adventures we've shared have spanned the universe— from my mansion in quiet Salem Center, New York, to the Shi'ar galaxy, through many bizarre dimensions of time and space in between.

And still our struggle against evil mutants, and intolerant humans bent on the destruction of all mutantkind, contin-

---

ues. Every day, it seems, some new force threatens humanity's well-being. And yet, I find I must take time between battles to reflect upon that which has come before, and to pay tribute to some of the greatest individuals I've ever known—my X-Men. I have also encouraged these dedicated heroes to record their most memorable adventures in their own words—not only to preserve these chronicles of courage, but in many cases to purge themselves of the pain that is part of a hero's burden.

CHAPTER 1

·······················

Professor X

I would never ask my X-Men to do anything I wouldn't do myself. So I will be the first to speak in this journal.

The great psychologist Sigmund Freud believed the man is shaped by the child; I agree that our early experiences direct our destinies. Therefore, I have chosen to describe a series of incidents from my youth that led me to my chosen career.

Many people go through their entire lives without ever feeling a "calling" to any particular profession. These events constitute my calling, and the reason I have dedicated my life's work and my inheritance to the founding of my School for Gifted Youngsters, the X-Men, and subsequent teams of mutant heroes.

```
file: therapeutic debriefing
subfile: Charles Xavier
codename: Professor X
password: Cain
```

A chemical blast destroyed my father's laboratory. His colleague, Dr. Marko, escaped alive. My father did not.

I remember the funeral: standing beside my mother in the pouring rain, watching the soil heaped on my father's grave turn to mud. My mutant ability to read minds had not yet fully revealed itself to me, but I did not trust Dr. Marko. I sensed he was lying when he told Mother that he would have gladly died to save Father.

Later, I sensed a dark purpose behind Dr. Marko's marriage to my mother. I knew he was only after Mother's wealth. I believe that when Mother realized this, she died of a broken heart.

I suffered more heartache in the form of my stepbrother, Cain Marko. The moment he walked through the mansion's large front door, I sensed Cain was sadistic and evil. He quickly proved me right. Though he was older and more powerfully built than I, Cain slapped me often—

just to "teach me a lesson."

One day, I stood outside the luxurious laboratory Dr. Marko had built with Mother's money. I heard Cain arguing with his father.

"If you want money, go out and earn it, as I did!" Dr. Marko shouted.

"I know how you earned it!" Cain spat. "It was no accident Xavier died at Alamogordo...!"

I felt as if my heart had stopped beating. Had Dr. Marko murdered my father? I stepped closer to the half-opened door and peered into the lab.

Marko grabbed his son and shook him, shrieking with rage. "Don't ever say that again as long as you live!"

My small, young body filled with righteous fury. This man had taken both my parents from me for his own selfish gain! I marched into the laboratory and demanded to know the truth.

"Cain—Cain doesn't know what he's saying," Dr. Marko stammered.

Cain glared at me. "I know plenty! And no bratty stepbrother is gonna cause trouble now!"

He swung at a nearby rack of test tubes. Marko shouted, "Cain! Don't touch them! They're explosive!"

Too late! In the strange slow motion of crisis,

I saw the chemicals spill and ooze toward each other, unstoppable as fate. *Ka-boom!*

The world around me shattered and burst into flames. My ears rang and my lungs filled with hot air laced with foul chemicals. Through my smoke-blurred eyes the floor seemed to rush up to meet me as I collapsed.

Cool air on my face revived me. Dr. Marko was carrying Cain and me to safety, despite his own mortal injuries. In halting gasps, Dr. Marko said, "Charles...your father's death was an accident! I might have saved him...if I tried. I did not...Please forgive me."

How could I not? In one gallant gesture, Dr. Marko had made up for his earlier cowardice and greed; he had given his life to save me, even though he had failed my father. Life, I have since learned, is full of such ironies, like my stepbrother's bearing the name of Abel's jealous, murdering brother.

To this day, I still shudder at Dr. Marko's final words, "Beware of...Cain! When he finds out about your power..."

Power? How could he know what I had only begun to suspect? But soon my simple ability to sense people's true natures developed into the awesome powers I term *psionics*, which allow me to move matter using only my mind and to read others' thoughts.

Almost as soon as my powers emerged, I realized they should be hidden lest they inspire the envy of others. The only outward sign of my powers was the premature loss of my hair. In the meantime, I continued to excel at everything—from academics to sports. Though I meant Cain no harm, each honor and trophy I earned in school was like a knife in his jealous heart.

One day he could bear it no longer. "Another trophy for you, skinhead?" Cain's cruel words startled me. I hadn't heard him enter the mansion's game room. I turned and saw Cain's face was a red mask of fury. I probed for the reason, but Cain's hatred was like a wall of flames preventing access to his rational mind. Since he had never applied himself to anything but tormenting others, Cain had no trophies of his own. And there I was, placing yet another of mine on the mantel.

"Get them outta here!" Cain raged.

He was out of control, a maddened bull charging the red flag of my achievements. Cain picked up a pool cue and smashed my trophies to shards. I knew I would be next, so before Cain could throw his first punch I knocked him out with a quick karate blow.

Later, Cain offered to drive me back to college. Hoping to restore normal relations, at the least, I accepted.

Cain floored the accelerator and the speeding auto whipped around hairpin turns. He laughed when I warned him to slow down. "I'll drive like this until you beg me to stop!"

With sickening clarity, I realized Cain was completely evil. He did not even seek his own happiness any more—he wanted only to destroy mine, to have power over me. Just as fury had twisted his features into an ugly mask, rage had twisted his very soul.

Then the car careered through a DETOUR sign and over a cliff! As the back wheels left the road, I telekinetically lifted Cain to safety. But there was no time to save myself!

In the split-second before impact, I surrounded myself with a psionic shield. I recall with horror that endless fall and the ghastly crunch of metal as the car crumpled around me.

Without my powers, I would surely have died instantly. As it was, my injuries were exten-

sive and painful. Yet I lived to fight beside Cain in the Korean War.

I vividly recall the boom of mortar shells—and the thunderous beat of Cain's fear, so strong in his mind that it echoed painfully in my own. I knew Cain was going to desert almost before he knew. As he fled the ravaged battlefield I shouted, "Come back, you fool! You'll be court-martialed!"

But Cain didn't even look back. My step-brother ran, and I followed him to the cave where he sought shelter, hoping to spare him the punishment and humiliation of a military trial.

I stopped inside the mouth of the cave, staring in disbelief. What had seemed like an ordinary stone cave was a mysterious ancient temple. The walls were painted midnight blue, with brilliant gold images of the sun and planets. In the center stood a statue so bizarre and magnificent that it took my breath away. Four times the size of a man and wrought in gleaming gold, the idol had a hook nose and flickering ruby eyes, like twin pools of blood, that granted it an eerie semblance of life. At its gigantic feet, a golden disk bore a huge, glowing ruby. My studies of ancient lore told me this could only be the legendary Temple of Cyttorak!

I saw Cain reach for the ruby, even as the ancient tales flashed through my mind. "Don't touch it!" I shouted. But like his father's warning, mine came too late.

As light poured from the gem, Cain held the mystical jewel and read aloud the sacred words inscribed on it.

Whosoever touches this gem shall possess the power of the Crimson Bands of Cyttorak! Henceforth, you who read these words shall become...forevermore...a human juggernaut.

Cain's voice echoed eerily off the cave's dark walls. The ruby in his hands dissolved in a blinding red glow, and though Cain's features were obscured by that uncanny light, I plainly saw him grow into a creature of awesome proportions, with a chest as thick as a mighty oak tree and muscles as big as boulders.

Fascinated, I stood rooted to the spot, until the clatter of falling stones alerted me to the cave's imminent destruction. I scrambled out, just before the cave collapsed in a rain of rubble.

Cain was buried alive. Buried, I knew, but not dead. For the Crimson Bands of Cyttorak possessed powerful magic. The juggernaut they created would not be so easily defeated. My step brother, once merely twisted by envy, had become a genuine monster.

And even as this terrible truth became clear to me, my life's mission became clear as well. I realized there were other people like Cain, whose jealousy, rage, and greed drove them to deeds of destruction. And I realized also there are others, born with special powers like my own, whose mutant abilities could protect humanity.

My stepbrother, Cain, taught me about evil. And, in a curious way, he also taught me about good. I believe we all have a purpose in the complex web of life. I had found mine—to lead the X-Men in their valiant battle against evil!

CHAPTER 2

Jean Grey

Jean Grey's parents brought her to me for help when she was suffering from a terrible trauma. Her best friend had literally died in her arms, and at that very moment Jean's mutant powers emerged.

Like me, Jean has the ability to enter the minds of others, send out force bolts of awesome magnitude, and to move matter telekinetically. In this case, ten-year-old Jean had shared her friend's mind during the girl's last moments on earth. The shock was too much for young Jean to bear.

Using my own psionic powers, I created walls within her sensitive young mind that would allow Jean to grow into her powers gradually. I only wish I could always be as successful at protecting Jean from the pain such powers can bring. Since I cannot, I am glad Jean had the courage to face the ultimate challenge—death—and eventual rebirth as...the Phoenix!

file: therapeutic debriefing
subfile: Jean Grey
codename: Marvel Girl
password: Phoenix

How can I describe the most painful and exhilarating experience of my life? The incident started on a secret government space station orbiting Earth. The X-Men had been kidnapped by Sentinels, giant mutant-killing robots under the command of Steven Lang. In a mad scheme to destroy us, Lang had created robot duplicates of the X-Men—putting us in the peculiar position of fighting ourselves! I still shudder when I recall the sight of Wolverine's adamantium claws tearing the guts out of...me!

Our battle left the station in ruins, with every life-support system failing. Lang's men evacuated in all but one of the station's lifepods. We found a pilot, Dr. Corbeau, in the only remaining shuttle. He calmly explained why we were all doomed.

"The only path to Earth is through an intense solar flare," Corbeau began. 'The flight computer is down and the cockpit is severely damaged. I could execute a manual reentry, but in the unshielded cockpit I'd die of radiation poisoning before we reached Earth's atmosphere. One of you might survive the flare, but you can't pilot the shuttle. We need someone who can do both—and there's no such animal."

I looked around the shuttle at the other members of the team—the bravest, finest people I'd ever known. *How many times had we faced death together?* I asked myself. Would this be the last? My own death did not frighten me as much as the prospect of a world without Nightcrawler, Storm, Colossus, Banshee, Wolverine—and my beloved Scott (Cyclops).

Suddenly I knew what I had to do. "I'll pilot the ship."

"Are you crazy, Jean?" Scott shouted. "Since when are you a qualified astronaut?"

"Since now!" I put my hand across Dr. Corbeau's forehead and initiated a telepathic link. Only experience could make me a great pilot, but by absorbing his knowledge I could bring the shuttle back to Earth in one piece. At least I had to try!

Scott shook me hard. "And how will you survive the solar flare?"

"My telekinetic powers will screen out the

radiation," I interrupted, not sure they actually would, but knowing it was our only hope.

"For how long?" Scott countered. "Even your powers can't handle that much..."

"They can handle this," I said, zapping him with a psionic bolt which knocked him cold.

The others knew why I'd done it, but that didn't stop them from taking up Scott's cause. "It's suicide, Jeanie!" Wolverine cried.

I didn't have time to argue. If I succeeded, I'd apologize later. If not... "Shut your mouth and get into the shielded passenger compartment—now! Before I lose my temper!" I told Wolverine.

At least Storm didn't try to change my mind. "May the goddess protect you," she said. Then she hugged me.

As Storm left the cockpit, I called after her, tears choking my voice. "A last favor, my friend? Would you...tell Scott...I loved him."

Then I swung into action. I patched the hull with my telekinetic powers. Next, I fired the rear thrusters, using my newly acquired knowledge of piloting, and eased the shuttle free of the station. According to the instruments, we had one minute until we reached the solar flare—and half an hour before we'd be free of its intense radiation field. I was scared. No, I was terrified. Yet there was nothing I could do but forge ahead!

In seconds I felt the flare's first heat. I activated my psionic shield, which was almost instantly strained nearly to the breaking point. *Hold on,* I told myself, *for the love of all you hold dear!*

I watched the control-panel clock. Twenty minutes. Twenty minutes is nothing when you're safe at home reading a book or chatting with a friend. Twenty minutes is an eternity when one of nature's most powerful forces is burning through every cell in your body.

Even as I struggled to maintain my psionic shield, part of my mind was with the other X-Men in the passenger compartment. I felt Scott's anguish, so acute that it doubled my own. But what could I do?

Dr. Corbeau's scientific mind recorded the data. *I've never seen rad-counts this high. Outside this shielded compartment we'd all be dead in seconds. Jean Grey is our only hope—and a slim one at best. It's a miracle she's lasted this long.* Some days it just doesn't pay to be able to read minds!

I didn't dare break concentration to look at the clock again. The entire cockpit glowed as if I were sitting in the center of a raging bonfire. I realized my telekinetic powers were no match for the sun's fury. I dimly remember screaming, "Dear Lord, hear my prayer...and help me! It hurts! *Scott!*"

Ultraviolet light clouded my eyes with cataracts. My body withered, organs bleeding, muscles collapsing. Then I sensed a light behind me and wondered briefly if the ship had caught fire. *No, not fire,* I reasoned, *an hallucination.* I felt myself floating free, and the terrible pain was suddenly gone.

I realized that I was dying. I would fail. My friends, Scott—we would *all* die! And the world would be glad to be rid of a few more mutants.

No! My lips could no longer form the words, but my mind raged. *No!* I refused to die while so much depended on me.

Then I heard a voice impossible to describe. It sounded like music in my mind. *Who...what are you?* I wondered.

And the voice replied, "The sum and substance of life and hope and dreams. I have known you, Jean Grey, from the moment of your birth...as I have known the universe. You cried out for aid. I heard. I came."

The light coalesced into the faceless, radiant form of a woman. What remained of my rational mind rebelled against such a fantastic vision. *This is crazy,* I thought. *I'm crazy.*

"No more so than any finite being confronting the infinite," the lyrical voice replied. "Your form is so fragile, child. How can you endure?"

I must! The thought resounded fiercely in my mind. *To save the X-Men...and—most especially— Scott.*

Then the form changed and Scott stood before me. My withered arms reached for him.

That image—cast from my very soul—oh, my love, the essence of my hopes and dreams—all that almost was...and will never be. My innermost yearning. How could you know?

The light-being once more resumed the shape of a faceless woman. "My consciousness and form on this plane of existence derive from your dominant emotions and memories."

This was too much for me. *Oh, great. You're a figment of my imagination.*

The light-being's form took on more detail. As it spoke, I recognized a familiar mass of wavy hair. "You jest—yet what is imagination, save the ability to conceive of that which is beyond reality? You are human, Jean Grey; I am of creation."

Then I knew for certain the form the strange being was taking. *You're becoming me!* I realized, staring into my own face for the second time on that strangest of all days. Only this was no robot duplicate but...but what?

"This form is but a shell and only for the present. Your own physicality is far closer to its transition than you realize."

Not dying then. The horrible truth sank in. *Already dead. Hanging on, barely, by force of will alone...What do you want from me?* I thought wearily.

"It is for you to name your heart's desire."

I shuddered with a premonition of disaster. *And I'll get my wish? That sounds too good to be true.*

"There is a price," the being admitted. She warned me that the fire she offered could burn as well as heal, and could never be extinguished. Yet, as she knew, I had no choice but to accept her offer if I was going to save the X-Men. With the last fading remnant of life still animating my exhausted, radiation-wracked body, I reached out for the hand that offered me new life.

Suddenly, I surged with vitality. I was not just alive—I was singing with the stars! Nothing I have ever felt before or since comes close to that sensation. In one instant I went from near-death to radiant life, and from a mere mutant to a being with power more awesome than the sun itself! The very music of the stars pulsed through my veins. I felt the resonance of every living thing in the galaxy. I was pure fire, the soul and spirit of life incarnate. I was...the Phoenix!

I looked down at the withered body that seconds before had been my painful prison. Inside it, a stubborn ember of life yet burned. I enclosed those frail remains in a healing cocoon, and then began my new life—not as Jean Grey, but as the most powerful elemental force the universe has known.

CHAPTER 3

Cyclops

I still vividly recall my excitement on reading the report of Scott Summers's powers. A sudden burst of energy blasted from his eyes, and a huge construction crane toppled toward a crowded street. A second blast from those amazing eyes, and the crane was destroyed before anyone could be hurt. But the terrified crowd turned on the mutant youth, who ran away.

I spared no effort to find him. As I had guessed, Scott's initial outburst was involuntary. The second revealed his character, his desire to protect humanity. I easily persuaded Scott to become the first student at my institute, Xavier School for Gifted Youngsters.

There, I saw Scott grow from well-meaning teenager to full-fledged hero. I also watched his romance with Jean Grey grow into a deep and abiding love. Without it, I doubt Earth would have survived the emergence of Dark Phoenix. But I'll let Scott describe those events himself.

file: therapeutic debriefing
subfile: Scott Summers
codename: Cyclops
password: loyalty

I'm sure many a divorce petition begins with one partner complaining that the other has "changed." Well, I certainly know what it's like to have the woman you love change before your very eyes. But I can also record what is today a more unusual story—of my standing by Jean Grey through all those changes, believing in her despite overwhelming evidence, and best of all, seeing that faith justified.

(Perhaps you'll think it odd, Professor, that what I've chosen to record is an adventure that more rightly belongs in Jean's biography. But where there is love, there is little separation, and I find this episode defined me as much as it did Jean. She also confided to me that she had intended herself to record her adventures as Dark Phoenix, but found the incidents too painful to detail. So here I go!)

Part of Jean's consciousness had been transferred to the Phoenix entity, which had also taken on Jean's physical appearance. So we all believed the Phoenix was Jean and that she had miraculously acquired awesome powers through her prolonged contact with the solar flare. (I now think that I was so eager for Jean to be all right that I ignored differences I might otherwise have noticed between Phoenix and the woman I love.)

In any case, Phoenix, as she now chose to call herself, was accepted as a member of the X-Men. And we were certainly glad to have her with us on our first journey to the Shi'ar galaxy! There we faced the demented Emperor D'Ken, whose crystal tesseract, essentially a concentrated black hole, would have swallowed the entire cosmos if Jean—I mean, Phoenix—had not neutralized it with her amazing powers.

Now that we had seen the awesome extent of those powers, Professor X, Jean and I were concerned. Was a mere human consciousness meant to direct such vast, cosmic power? But if anyone could handle it, I figured, it was Jean.

And she might have, if not for our old enemy Mastermind, whose specialty is altering our perception of reality. He'd always been obsessed with Jean, and this time he was determined to imprison her in an elaborate fantasy world keyed into her own psyche. To do so, he used a fiendish mind-tampering device that released Jean's dark side, the suppressed desires that lurk in everyone's subconscious.

The Phoenix eventually rid herself of Mastermind's control, but she could not free herself from the darkness within. Once released, the dark side of Phoenix took over. Now it was virtue's turn to be repressed. And the Phoenix became Dark Phoenix.

Jean's loves and loyalties were lost within that blazing entity whose lust for power pitted her against the X-Men! The battle raged one dark night in New York City's Central Park. Bolts of pure energy crackled from Dark Phoenix in electron showers that dimmed even the lights of that great metropolis.

We could not help but pull our punches against someone we still believed to be our friend—and, in my case, much more. But Dark Phoenix batted us around as pitilessly as a cat toying with a mouse. Even the mighty Colossus was no match for Dark Phoenix.

Storm begged her to stop before someone got killed. "We are your friends! Let us help you— please!"

The Phoenix's reply nearly broke my heart. "It is too late for help, Ororo. For me, for you— for the universe. Dark Phoenix has no friends."

I felt for a moment as if the woman I loved was gone, replaced by this flaming demon. Yet the spark of hope inside me would not let go, even as it guttered like a candle in the wind.

I fought Dark Phoenix for the sake of the rest of the team, more than myself. But there was nothing any of us could do against her limitless powers.

"I didn't want this, my dear ones," Dark Phoenix said as she left us lying helpless on the ground. "But by striking you down, I free myself of the last ties binding me to the person I was, the life I led. Good-bye forever, X-Men. My destiny now lies in the stars!"

As Dark Phoenix spoke those words, I saw grief, deep as an ocean of tears, flicker across those familiar features. *Oh, Jean, I know you're in there! But how do I reach you?*

What happened next is a nightmare from which Jean will never fully recover. I believe that if anyone had the moral and psychical strength to restrain Dark Phoenix, it would have been Jean—and I maintain that she cannot be held responsible for the entity's actions. Forgive me, love, I must tell the tale.

A voracious, evil hunger sent Dark Phoenix far into space. There she dove into the very heart of a star much like our own sun, and consumed all the star's energy in just minutes.

And on the populated planet orbiting that sun, billions of peaceful citizens looked up into a suddenly dark sky and knew their doom. With as little thought as we might give to eating an apple, Dark Phoenix had devoured the star that gave them life—and killed an entire planet.

At the time, I didn't know what she had done. I only knew, through the telepathic link Jean and still I shared, that Dark Phoenix was returning to Earth—and she was still hungry!

My heart seized with dread. Would the X-Men have to kill Dark Phoenix to stop her...and could we? And what of the kind, good woman I could still feel hidden inside that ferocious shell of ultimate power?

Since we clearly lacked the ability to face the entity in direct combat, Beast used his scientific expertise to create a device designed to even the odds—a mind scrambler that would neutralize Dark Phoenix's power. We caught up with her outside Jean's parents' home. I believe that the part of Jean's consciousness inhabiting Dark Phoenix went there to prepare itself for the struggle yet to come. But though it may have been Jean's will that brought Dark Phoenix to her childhood home, it was most certainly Dark Phoenix who flew out the window to meet us.

While Storm rolled in a dense fog, Nightcrawler teleported behind Dark Phoenix and barely managed to slip the mind-scrambling headband over her auburn hair. The headband dampened her powers, but they were far from gone. Dark Phoenix fought the device with furious strength! We all tried to reason with Jean, but wound up fighting Dark Phoenix.

Wolverine came closest to victory. I remember his hesitating over Dark Phoenix's huddled form, adamantium claws poised to strike. "Forgive me, darlin'," he said.

"D-do it, Wolverine!" the woman begged. "Strike while the human part of me is still in control. I beg you...I don't want to hurt you!"

I felt as if I'd been torn in half. Jean was in there! Good, noble Jean, who would rather die than hurt her friends. I held my breath. Would Wolverine deliver the final blow?

He never had a chance. Dark Phoenix threw him off and tore the burned-out scrambler from her head. "That was an admirable ploy, X-Men. But a ploy that failed!"

Then she encased the team in an energy field—preparing for what, I do not know. I chose that moment to step forward and play my last card.

"Have you come to fight?" Dark Phoenix asked when she saw me. Her eyes glowed with cosmic power.

"I came to talk," I replied.

"I won't listen," she said with a sneer.

"Then kill me," I countered. And at that moment, I would rather have died than live another day without my Jean. "Kill me," I dared. "If you can. But if you can't, ask yourself why."

"You're not worth killing," Dark Phoenix spat. Yet her slight hesitation revealed that she knew this answer was false.

"You can't kill any of us," I said. "Because you love us, and we love you."

"Dark Phoenix knows nothing of love," she said bitterly.

"Oh? For love of the X-Men you sacrificed your life. For love of me, you resurrected yourself from a burnt cinder into the Phoenix entity. For love of the universe you risked your life again to save humanity from the Shi'ar Emperor's crystal." I only hoped my words would reach her. "Jean, you are love!"

I watched the battle of emotions across Jean's beautiful face. One instant it was Jean's face, the next Dark Phoenix's.

"Your existence, your very creation, springs from love, the noblest of human emotions. And now you want to deny that?" I asked.

"Yes!" she cried. And a second later, "No!" Then she struggled to explain. "I...hunger, Scott—for a joy, a rapture, beyond all comprehension. That need is a part of me, too. It consumes me."

"It doesn't have to. Trust me!" I begged. "Let me help—"

Suddenly the woman before me was turned to living fire. She shrieked in pain. "Jean!" I shouted.

Professor X had sneaked up on us and blasted Dark Phoenix with his most powerful psionic bolt. For a moment, Dark Phoenix had seemed almost ready to trust me and now...I was furious! "What have you done?"

"While you distracted her, I was able to attack. I had no alternative," the Professor explained. "Now stand aside. I do not want you to be hurt."

Dark Phoenix turned to me, face blazing with fury. "You heard our 'mentor,' my love. Away with you!"

And with a powerful blast she sent me flying. Then she embarked upon a ferocious psionic battle with Professor X.

The heavens themselves were moved by the titanic play of forces as one awesome mind battled another, holding nothing back. Then came a blast as brilliant as a star gone nova. And the body that had held the Dark Phoenix entity collapsed in my arms.

I held my breath for what seemed like an eternity. Was she dead? Could I go on without her? Had Professor X saved the world—but killed the love of my life?

I looked down at the woman in my arms. Long lashes fluttered, the lids opened to reveal two beautiful green eyes. I stared deep into those emerald pools and felt my pulse quicken with joy. It was Jean, my Jean!

Professor X could hardly believe his victory,

since his powers are not nearly as great as those of the Dark Phoenix. But we both knew the reason. Jean's love, for me and for the other X-Men, had tipped the scales in that fateful battle—just as it has given meaning to my life.

CHAPTER 4

·······················

Wolverine

Logan's skeleton is reinforced with adamantium, a super-strong metal, which renders his limbs nearly unbreakable. In addition, he possesses retractable claws in his forearms, bonded with adamantium, that can be extended at will like the claws of a cat. Logan is also endowed with the ability to heal himself quickly from wounds that would kill an ordinary human. These superhuman attributes, combined with Logan's superior combat skills, make him a formidable opponent. Once unleashed, his battle frenzy recalls the famed berserkers of Norse myths.

Yet, although he is as ferocious as the small predator whose name he shares, Wolverine also possesses a tender side. He is fluent not only in English, but in Japanese, Russian, Spanish, Cheyenne, and Lakota, and is a great appreciator of Japanese culture. Though he may seem a wild animal to some, Logan is capable of humanity's highest emotion, love, which is the subject he discusses here.

I like talking into a machine about as much as having to put out my cigar in an elevator, but here goes, bub. This is the story of the toughest and best battle I ever fought—a battle for love.

Now I couldn't just fall for the girl next door. That'd be too easy. Me, I fell like a ton of bricks for the daughter of one of the oldest, noblest, richest, most powerful clans in Japan. And here's the punchline: Mariko Yashida actually fell in love with me, too. Ain't life a crock?

'Course, if it wasn't for bad luck I'd have no luck at all, so you can bet things didn't go smoothly. Sure, Mariko loved me, but suddenly my letters to her started coming back unopened, and my phone calls went unanswered.

I flew to Japan to find out the score and guess what? Mariko was married. My Mariko! Turns out her father, Shingen, who'd been presumed dead for years, showed up to reclaim leadership of the Yashida clan. And he came with some debt that was paid with Mariko's hand in marriage. I know honor is sacred to the Japanese, but I also knew I loved Mariko, and that meant nobody should marry her but me!

I reached the Yashida home by midnight. It was more of a fortress than a home—huge stone towers topped with flat, pagoda-style roofs. I climbed the cold stone, sniffing the air but catching no scent of guards. The night was too quiet, too still.

I got inside the dark house with no trouble, which made me even more suspicious. Then I forgot everything because the scent of jasmine reached me on the cool breeze. Mariko! I followed the perfume to find her in the garden, praying before a gigantic, moonlit statue of Buddha.

I wish I could say she was glad to see me, but she wasn't. Without even turning to look at me, Mariko said what was between us was over.

"At least have the courage to face me," I growled.

She turned, and white-hot rage boiled through me. Purple, swollen bruises marred one eye and cheek. What beast could do this to someone as gentle and kind as Mariko? My fists clenched and through gritted teeth I said,

"Mariko, come with me. Any court in the land will grant you a divorce."

"I will not ask for one," she said.

Then I said the words that come easy only around her. "I love you!"

"And I...you. But I am bound by far more important obligations."

The argument was interrupted by the arrival of her husband, a little weasel-faced, four-eyed geek who shrieked, "Mariko! You were told to await me in our apartments. If you are determined to defy me, wife, I must continue to punish you until you learn your proper place."

I grabbed him by the skinny neck and lifted him off the floor with one hand. Adamantium claws snicked out of the other, but Mariko stopped me before I could strike. In her quiet way she's as stubborn as I am—and I could deny her nothing.

So I left, but I didn't get far. A few feet down the rice-papered hall I heard a faint whistling and before my eyes could focus on the speeding metal stars, five ninja *shuriken* hit me from nowhere.

There had been no guards, I realized, because this was a trap. Blacking out, I thought: *Poison.*

Deadly. But not for me. Being a mutant has its advantages.

I came to feeling like the punching bag in Sugar Ray Leonard's gym, and guess who was smiling down at me from between two sumo wrestlers? Shingen Yashida. Some guys you just gotta hate on sight. Mariko and the weasel were there, too, but Shingen was the one who challenged me to a duel. He tossed me a wooden practice sword because, he said, I wasn't worthy of steel.

We took a few whacks at each other, and then Shingen started cheating. He went for the vulnerable nerve points where a blow could cripple—or kill. But worse than that, the guy was good—old, but a master at the top of his form. His wooden sword sang through the air and pounded the nerve cluster on one side of my neck. My counterstrike was slowed by the poison. He struck the other side of my neck— hard!

Shingen left me no choice. I popped my claws. My eyes flickered over to Mariko and my heart sank. She didn't realize her father was striking me with killing blows. She only saw my claws come out and thought I was the one being dishonorable.

I knew I had to hurt the old snake or die. But my heart wasn't in the attack, and my claws caught the cloth of his kimono, not flesh. Shingen's response was swift and savage. His sword hit my spine so hard I felt like I was going to snap in two. My legs went numb. His sword smashed into my throat. I tried to breathe, but spat blood instead—and from there it just got worse.

"Behold, daughter, the 'man' you love is not a man at all, but an animal. Witness his true nature. Is he such a prize?" Shingen taunted.

I saw Mariko's beautiful, bruised face. Her answer sounded like a death sentence. "No." Shingen leapt at me—and everything went black.

I woke up in an alley just off the busy Ginza. Anyone else would've been dead. I wished I was. But that didn't last long. I'm not the kind who gives up. What's the old saying? Where there's life, there's hope. And somehow I had to hope that I could get Mariko back.

As soon as I could walk again, I was sniffing around the edges of Shingen's empire. Like I figured, the old snake was up to his neck in

crime. He had a finger in every gambling house, drug gang, and vice trap in Japan. He must've spent years building up his organization. I ripped it to shreds in a few crazy days—shaking down one scumbag at a time. I left my signature at each stop, till I was ready to issue my final challenge: TONIGHT.

Either he'd die or I would. Either way, it wouldn't be pretty. But it would be over. Shingen had made this into something bigger than me and Mariko. It was about right and wrong, about freeing a country I love almost as much as my own from a man who does not deserve to rule its people.

The Yashida fortress brooded like a darker patch of night in the sky. Shingen's guards went down fast, or maybe I was just so mad the job came easy.

I padded down the hall, expecting anything and everything to jump at me from behind the rice-paper screens. I smelled jasmine, then turned a shadowed corner and saw ol' weasel neck dragging Mariko down the hall. His fear stank even at that distance. "Forget about your father," he said. "You're coming with me."

Mariko cried, "No!"

Her husband grunted, "No arguments."

That's when I saw he was holding a gun. What coward's complete without one?

"You heard the lady, bub," I told him. "She wants to stay."

Then the weasel put the gun to Mariko's head. "One false move, Wolverine, and she dies! Now step into the light, where I can see you."

I did as he said, even though I knew he'd shoot me. The bullet missed, but Shingen's ninja didn't. Ol' weasel-neck was as dead as Aunt Martha's mink stole, with three spikes poking out of his back. I figured the big man himself wanted to see me, and that was just fine with me!

I found Shingen in a room filled with Samurai armor. Shadows from the wood-framed *shoji* screens cut the floor and walls into squares of dark and light.

"Am I worthy of steel now?" I called.

Shingen pulled the metal blade of the Yashida clan honor sword from its ornamented sheath. The blade hissed like a cobra. I unsheathed my claws.

"That remains to be seen!" Shingen shouted, and we both leapt, blades singing through the air. We passed each other in mid-flight. My claws cut, but his sword cut deeper. Hot blood ran down my side, but the night breeze carried Mariko's jasmine scent and I was ready to fight!

Shingen was fast and deadly as before. But this time I knew what I was fighting for. His sword was a blur of steel. All I could do was dodge and block, and then he stabbed me through the side.

Pain meant nothing to me. I was too angry for pain. His slight smile revealed that Shingen thought the fight was over. He withdrew his sword and placed it by my neck to strike the killing blow.

My claws retracted. I grabbed the sword and pulled him close. His evil face leered at me like a Kabuki mask. *Snikt!* Out came the claws, and down went Shingen. It was over.

Mariko's shadow fell through the open doorway. "Father," she said.

I wondered if I'd lost her forever. Honor and duty would demand that we be enemies till death. And I knew when it came to honor, Mariko had the strength of a tigress.

Mariko picked up her father's honor sword. I would rather die than raise a hand against her. If she killed me, so be it!

"This sword represents the Yashida clan—all we were and are and wish to be," Mariko said. "It is to be worn not by the leader of the clan, but by the samurai who best exemplifies those qualities."

Then she handed me the sword.

I was stunned by the honor she offered me. I stammered, "I am...unworthy."

"You fought for the good of others, for right and truth; my father only fought for greed and survival. You fought though you believed it would cost you everything you held dear. And thereby, beloved, you proved you are what my father could never hope to be."

I guess I pretty much stopped hearing after the word *beloved*. Mariko was mine! I put my battered arms around her and kissed her. And I ain't much for sentimental moments, but you might as well know that was the happiest moment of my whole crazy life.

Fightin' the good fight's not all parades and cigars, but sometimes the good guys do win. Sometimes they even get the girl.

Unfortunately, guys like me know two things about good times; there are never enough of them, and they don't last.

CHAPTER 5

Rogue

Rogue enrolled in my school after being a member of the second Brotherhood of Evil Mutants, whose amoral members exploit their special powers for no higher purpose than greed. Rogue's powers include a unique capacity to absorb, through skin-to-skin contact, the abilities, memories, and very identity of others.

At the command of the Brotherhood's leader, Mystique, Rogue absorbed the powers of Carol Danvers, a.k.a. Ms. Marvel. To Rogue's dismay, the usually temporary transfer of identity in this case was permanent. As the two personalities warred within her, Rogue discovered that to Mystique she was merely a useful tool. When she needed help, Rogue found herself utterly alone.

She came to me. And though the X-Men strongly favored turning our enemy out (and worse) I chose to use the opportunity to school a vulnerable young mind toward good and away from evil. I have never regretted that decision.

file: therapeutic debriefing
subfile: Rogue
codename: Rogue
password: dues paid

When Ah first joined the X-Men Ah felt about as welcome as a skunk at a picnic. (Ah can't blame them, really. After all, Ah'd almost killed their friend, Carol Danvers.) But the Professor gave me a chance to prove myself. Ah fought beside the X-Men for a long time, but Ah never truly belonged until we all went to Japan for Wolverine's wedding.

Ah remember standing in the doorway of that luxurious apartment watching Wolverine hug the others who had made the trip: Colossus, Nightcrawler, Shadowcat, and Storm. With his keen senses, Wolverine must have smelled us all coming a block away. But he pretended not to know Ah was there. And that hurt.

Then Wolverine's beautiful fiancée, Lady Mariko, said, "Logan-san. One of the X-Men remains outside. Will you not invite her in?"

Wolverine's voice went through me, sharp as his adamantium claws. "If it were up to me, I'd cut out her heart."

Storm stood up for me. "Professor Xavier has accepted Rogue as an X-Man. We all have."

"Figures. Any outfit that'll take me as a member'll admit anyone," Wolverine muttered.

Ah was about to pick up mah suitcase and hightail it outta there when Mariko said, "You judge yourself and your comrades too harshly, Wolverine." Then she took both mah hands in hers and said, "Welcome, Rogue-san. May your stay with us be a happy one."

Ah can't tell y'all what her words meant to me. Ah was almost too grateful to speak mah thanks. Folks may say Southern hospitality is the finest, but in mah mind that Far Eastern lady will always be the height of graciousness.

But don't get me wrong. Mariko wasn't all lace and doilies. Since her daddy's death, she was the leader of one of the most powerful families in Japan. Unfortunately, Lady Mariko's daddy had ties with organized crime, and as Ah well know, once you're in the underworld it's hard to break free. To make matters worse, Mariko's half-brother, Harada—a.k.a. the Silver Samurai—was tearing up Tokyo trying to grab control of that clan for himself. Why, it was just as mixed up as a hillbilly feud!

'Course, the Silver Samurai wasn't the only one wanting his slice of the Tokyo pie. This mean green lady known as Viper slithered into Mariko's house that night and spiked our tea with deadly poison. Ah guess she figured the only way she could take out Lady Mariko was if she got the X-Men out of the way first.

But Wolverine detected the poison in time to get us all to the hospital. Mah mutant physique was barely affected by it. Same with Wolverine, who vowed to bring down Lady Mariko's enemies that night!

"Ah'm coming with you, Wolverine," Ah declared in the hall outside the Intensive Care Unit.

Wolverine glared at me. "No way."

But he's not the only stubborn one. Ah said, "You need backup, and Ah'm all you've got."

Wolverine slammed open the swinging doors so hard I thought they'd pull off their hinges, and he growled, "Okay, kid. But you follow my lead—every flamin' step o' the way."

We rattled some cages on the bad side of Tokyo, and shook loose some rats. One told us where to find a man named Nabatone, a crime boss with connections to both the Silver Samurai and Viper. We figured he was the man to see.

Nabatone lived in a lavish estate outside Tokyo. Even by faint moonlight Ah could tell the grounds were beautiful—all rock gardens, bonsai, and sweet cherry blossoms. But at the time Ah was more concerned with the computer-controlled defenses. One false step and the whole place would be crawling with guards.

Ah lifted Wolverine over the electronic sensors. (He may be short, but he sure is heavy!) He didn't exactly say thanks, but Ah could tell he was thinking Ah'd at least proven myself useful.

We got inside the house with no trouble, which made Wolverine suspicious. Heck, he's always suspicious. That's what comes of a life-time of fighting.

Being invulnerable to most forms of attack, Ah wasn't scared. So Ah took a moment to admire mah surroundings. (It ain't every day a little girl from Mississippi gets to see a beautiful Japanese home.) Ah had to appreciate the sleek simplicity of the sliding rice-paper walls supported by panes of light wood, the rooms that lacked clutter or even furniture. A lone statue of Buddha dominated the entrance room.

"Stay close and quiet and follow my lead,"

Wolverine whispered. He crouched along the floor like a prowling animal.

I walked upright, unconcerned. "Sho' nuff, boss." Mah voice echoed loudly in the emptiness.

"You think we're playin' games, kid?"

Ah could tell Wolverine was mad. "Nosiree. Ah'm just not afraid of being hurt," Ah explained airily. "Comes with being invulnerable."

Wolverine sniffed the air. "Someone's downstairs, alone."

"Let's get the sucker!" Ah cried. Wolverine ain't the only one who enjoys a good fight! But before Ah could take another step, Wolverine kicked the feet right out from under me!

"Hey!" Ah shouted, as we landed together on the hard floor. Ah was about to ask, "What'd you do that for?" when the answer exploded in front of mah face. Activated by a sensor Ah'd tripped, a laser blew the serene Buddha to smithereens.

"Next time watch your step. That statue could've been you," Wolverine growled.

Ah was grateful and a little flustered— Wolverine cared! But Ah didn't like being talked down to like a child. And Ah guess Ah wanted to

remind him of mah power, so Ah leaned down as if to kiss mah hero. Ah was going to stop before touching his face, of course, but Wolverine's fist met mah chin first! But he didn't unsheathe his fancy claws, or Ah wouldn't be talkin' into this gadget, now would Ah?

"Don't ever pull a stunt like that again!" Wolverine hissed.

Ah knew right away Ah'd made a mistake. Ah'd just wanted to make a joke, but Ah'd gone and reminded him of what I'd done to his friend Carol—and why he hated me so much.

"Ah didn't mean no harm!" Ah protested.

"That's why you're still breathing," Wolverine replied, and he went right back to the mission without giving me any more thought than a cow gives a caterpillar. Ah followed him, forcing mah mind to the task at hand. After all, more nasty ol' booby traps might spring from the rice-paper walls.

We found Nabatone sitting by himself, looking like he was asleep. Wolverine smelled the strange smell before I did, and tried to keep me from entering the rush-matted room while he examined the man in the elegant kimono.

"Nabatone joined his ancestors over a week

ago," Wolverine said. "We've been suckered! While we're out here in the boondocks chasin' smoke, the Silver Samurai and Viper have a clean shot at Mariko and the X-Men!"

Ah felt sick to mah stomach—not from the smell, but from the thought of something happening to Wolverine's lovely lady. Ah guess ah don't have to tell you we were back at that hospital in a flash!

Soon as we rounded the corner of the hall leading to the Intensive Care Unit, we spotted a squad of ninjas led by Viper—green as a garden snake from her hair to her toes and cold as ice. "I want no witnesses, no survivors." Her green-tinted lips twisted in an evil grin.

"That ain't very sociable, Viper honey," Ah said sweetly. Then Ah grabbed two of those ninjas and flung them through a plate glass window with a satisfying *Smash!*

While Ah taught Viper's ninjas some manners, Wolverine took out the Silver Samurai. When Ah caught up with him outside the I.C.U., he was by his lady love's side. And Viper was aiming a laser gun right at his heart!

Viper fired the gun and Ah saw that big ol' laser beam streak straight for Wolverine and

Mariko! Ah flew faster than Ah knew Ah could and shoved the love-birds aside.

"Take a hike, shorty!" Ah said. Wolverine started to protest, but mah shove was already sending him and Mariko flying through the stairwell door. (Oops! Ah guess Ah pushed 'em a bit hard.)

Then Ah felt the laser beam blast into me. It was like a hot fist punching mah chest.

"A noble gesture, X-Man. I hope your compeers appreciate your sacrifice," Viper hissed, still firing the brilliant blast of heat and light and killing energy at me full force.

"Joke's on you, lady. They don't care if Ah live or die!" Ah shouted through the pain. Ah was determined to take the hit, whatever happened, to pay back Mariko's kindness to me.

Ah didn't know if ah could take any more when the laser suddenly stopped. Ah saw Viper throwing aside the glowing, overloaded gun. Ah guess she found out the hard way you shouldn't fire a laser at full blast for that long. Viper tele-ported her sneaky self outta there just as ah collapsed in Wolverine's arms.

"Ah guess Ah ain't as invulnerable as Ah thought," Ah gasped. It seemed sorta funny to be dying, kinda like a rude surprise.

"Don't talk stupid, kid. My healing factor can save you." Wolverine's voice was choked with emotion.

"No! You need that to save yourself," Ah said. Messed up as Ah was, Ah could tell that between the poison and the battle, Wolverine was in no shape to save anyone. Ah couldn't let him do that, especially not for an old enemy like me. "If Ah absorb your powers, you might die."

"My risk," he said. And the last thing Ah remember as Ah faded to black was feeling his healing factor flow into me.

And Ah guess y'all know by now we both made it. So that's how little ol' Rogue lived to become a true member of the X-Men. That's the story, sugah, unless you want to hear more!

CHAPTER 6

Beast

As the amazingly powerful mutant Beast, Hank McCoy embodies the best of animal and man. Watching him tumble, climb, and swing reminds one of nature's most accomplished acrobats—our evolutionary cousins, the great apes.

Yet Hank's brutish physique houses one of the most brilliant minds it has ever been my pleasure to meet. Hank is vastly accomplished in his chosen career of biochemistry, and his knowledge extends to many other fields as well. He is one of the most widely read individuals I have ever known, with a sense of humor as dry as French champagne.

People who judge a man by his appearance assume Hank is a wild animal, never suspecting the supreme intelligence lurking beneath the fur. What can it be like to look like a beast, but be a man? Each day Hank lives in the twilight zone between what appears to be and what is. So it does not surprise me that he has chosen this experience to discuss here.

file: therapeutic debriefing
subfile: Henry "Hank" McCoy
codename: Beast
password: human

I did not have as difficult a time growing up as many of my mutant friends. For one thing, my powers—superhuman agility and tremendous intelligence—have been with me since birth. They did not erupt, as some others' have, along with the pimples and painful changes of adolescence. My classmates might have stared at my big hands and feet, the only outward signs of my mutant status at the time, but they certainly did not object to my prowess on the football field. I learned to accept my difference, to appreciate and use its advantages.

Subsequent to my school days, while employed as a genetic researcher at Brand Chemicals, I created a formula I hoped would change my slightly odd appearance enough to permit me to perform undercover work against enemy spies. The serum worked rather differently than anticipated. My mutant powers increased, but my appearance was permanently altered.

If you think finding size 20 shoes is a challenge, try blending with the crowd when you are covered in blue fur! But I adapted because, as Darwin observed of everything from goldfinches to chimpanzees, that is what living creatures do.

I even found a female companion who could get past the fur to the man inside. But, alas, my romance with Vera Gantor was not in the stars. As many a poet has observed, love is rare and lasting love is rarer still—especially when your busy schedule includes making the world safe for both humans and mutants.

At least, such was the lofty goal espoused by myself and the other founding members of X-Factor, an organization we created when the X-Men disbanded after the disappearance of Professor X. (Though presumed dead, the good Professor was actually receiving intensive medical treatment in the Shi'ar galaxy, where the technology is far more advanced than that available on Earth.)

In any case, since X-Factor headquarters were then located on the Hudson River, whose tainted waters touch Manhattan's west side, I decided to find an apartment nearby. And, since my pockets were not nearly as deep as Donald Trump's, a roommate seemed advisable, and fellow X-Factor member Iceman, a.k.a. young Robert Drake, volunteered.

If ever a town deserved the title role in Charles Dickens's classic *Tale of Two Cities*, it is New York: the best of towns and the worst of towns. Exciting, sophisticated, bustling capital of art and industry; center for crime, filth, and social inequity.

On our first day of apartment-hunting, Robert and I were biting the wormy end of the Big Apple. We'd just seen a charming little $1000-a-month walkup with hot and cold running cockroaches when I decided it was time to pay a call on Vera. My erstwhile lady love's latest communiqués indicated that she, too, had settled in the world's most wonderful and terrible town.

We had barely sipped our herbal tea when Vera's apartment started shaking and a gigantic man in violet tights burst through the wall shouting, "I've looked for you a long time, furball! Now get ready to be smashed by *Tower!*"

At first I thought I was somehow dreaming. But since my dreams don't usually rock the room, I quickly realized this behemoth was real! I immediately instructed Iceman to protect Vera while I handled Twinkletoes.

"Don't worry about them, Bigfoot. You're the only one I'm after," the purple-clad mutant boomed.

"Handsome men like me are always in demand. But I'll decline your kind invitation," I replied, while my mind raced in confusion. Who was this being and what could he want with me? There wasn't time to find out. I was thoroughly engaged in the all-consuming business of having my lights extinguished one punch at a time. Apparently Tower had superhuman strength to match his superhuman size.

I came to with my wrists chained to the wall of a cell, and looking into the face of a man I'd thought was dead.

Carl Maddicks had been my colleague during my Brand Chemicals days. He was partly responsible for the serum injection which had enhanced my powers while rendering me blue and furry. Now, apparently, Maddicks had employed Tower to kidnap me in order to obtain my assistance in an experiment to reverse the process, to change me from *homo superior* to *homo sapiens,* from mutant to man.

Naturally, I refused to cooperate. Call me a

spoilsport, but I do not like being kidnapped—and I certainly wouldn't trust a kidnapper to use such a powerful formula for good and not evil.

Carl left me alone in my small padded cell to reconsider my decision. I confess that with nothing to distract my mind, I brooded over my situation. Bad enough to look like a beast, but now I was caged like a zoo animal!

In his dialogues with Plato, Socrates called man's life a prison from which he had no right to escape. Richard Lovelace's famous poem declares, "Stone walls do not a prison make, nor iron bars a cage..." But I was finding little consolation in philosophy or poetry.

I was rapidly running out of prison-themed quotes with which to divert myself. My mind, even more than my body, cried out for exercise. So when Carl tossed a copy of his research through the door, I pounced on the pages.

How could I know that as I read the work and corrected Carl's sloppy formulae in my mind, his mutant son, Arthur, was in the next room reading my thoughts? I had unwittingly helped my captor...and nearly sealed my own doom!

Using my corrected equations, Carl quickly prepared a serum and, without regard to proper

testing procedures or controls, immediately injected me. As I lay in a haze of pain and nausea, he confessed the reason for his actions. Carl's young son had developed mutant powers, but also, along with them, severe physical deformities. Carl was desperate to cure his son—and I was both assistant and guinea pig.

The agony that followed is painful even to recall. I suffered a heart attack during one phase of the experiment and nearly died.

I was unconscious when the other members of X-Factor hunted down Tower and forced from him all the sordid details of my capture. They rescued me and young Arthur from the laboratory, but Carl lost his life in the enusing battle. Of course, X-Factor, whose raison d'être is to provide aid to all mutants, was more than happy to offer Arthur a new home. The poor boy had never wanted his father to hurt me and was delighted to live among other people—mutants—like himself. I awoke days later in X-Factor's medical laboratory, feeling like a mummy. I couldn't wait to have the bandages removed.

My first sight as the gauze was peeled away was the gaping faces of my companions: Iceman,

Angel, Jean Grey, and Cyclops.

"Holy..." Iceman gasped.

"Will you look at that?" Angel marveled.

"I don't believe it!" Jean exclaimed.

They had done an excellent job of teasing my curiosity. "Well, how do I look?"

Iceman's next remark did nothing to elucidate the matter. "Like a roadie for the Talking Heads."

Jean hugged me. "I don't care how you look! Just as long as you're back with us!"

I soon realized the only opinion I could trust was my own. A quick glance in the mirror determined that I looked...human!

There were, unfortunately, side effects. I soon discovered that, along with my blue fur, I had lost a good measure of my intelligence. I knew isolated facts, but could not piece them together coherently. Some things I knew, but did not understand why. Words, which have always delighted me, on and off the printed page, eluded me like ghosts.

For instance, I knew that Iceman's new girlfriend, Infectia, was a dangerous mutant. (One kiss would have killed him!) But try as I might, I simply could not explain it to him! My friend's life was at stake, yet I could not find the words to help him. The frustration was nearly unbearable!

In the end, though, Carl's serum proved to be unstable. Once again, I hovered between life and death, between mutant and man. This time, Cyclops watched over me as I lay in agony, strapped to the examining table in the laboratory on X-Factor's new sentient homebase, named Ship. He could not hide his astonishment as my flesh repeatedly changed from blue fur to human skin and back again.

Neither Cyclops nor Ship knew how to help me. The ship interrupted Cyclops's vigil with a video news broadcast from New York City, where Jean and Iceman were chaperoning the youngest members of X-Factor—children like Arthur Maddicks whose mutant powers had forced them from their families.

Through my spasms I saw some familiar faces on the ship's TV screen. In the crowd of onlookers were Jean, Robert, and the children. And they were staring at Tower—the man who had kidnapped me! Tower, it seems, was declaring himself a member of a militant mutant group called the Alliance of Evil.

"We're gonna teach the city what mutants

can do—especially mondo mad mutants," he growled.

"We challenge X-Factor to try and stop us," taunted one of his companions.

Though racked with convulsions, I somehow managed to watch the screen. As Arthur and the other youngsters stood frozen in terror, Jean Grey and Iceman flew into action against several evil mutants. Tower grabbed Iceman and another villain seized Jean.

A volatile mixture of emotions boiled in me: Anger, frustration, concern for my companions. Suddenly the ship's restraints could hold me no more. Strength coursed through my veins and the clouds cleared from my mind!

"Ship! Restrain him!" Cyclops commanded as I sprang to my feet.

The ship's mechanical voice replied, "He has grown too strong! I am currently not able..."

"Cyclops! Don't worry!" I assured X-Factor's leader. "I'm okay." And as I spoke the words, I realized I was.

I saw...or heard, that Jean and the kids were in deep trouble with the Alliance. I needed to help them! I looked down at myself and realized...I was blue again, and furry...a monster to some. But humanity is measured in mind and soul, not the number of hair follicles, and I could reason again! Oh...the joy of language...the ecstasy of ideas! But I decided to reserve finesse for those who require it. Brute strength would suffice against the Alliance. And that I had in abundance! Now, with the aid of a teleportation beam from Ship I could get to my friends!

I was on the scene in an instant, with my mutant abilities back to form. And as my flippant friend Wolverine might say, I kicked evil mutant posterior.

So there you have it, my adventures as man and beast. I can only speculate that there is a God—and that he just couldn't stand the thought of me being so smart and handsome, too. Joking aside, perhaps some things were just meant to be. I leave the philosophizing to you, Professor. Personally, I'd rather read a good book.

CHAPTER 7

Storm

Since the dawn of humanity, Ororo Munroe's female ancestors have been distinguished by white hair, blue eyes, and exceptional powers. My mutant-detecting computer, Cerebro, helped me locate Ororo on Africa's Serengeti Plain where, like her ancestors, she lived as a witch-priestess. The local tribes had given her the name Beautiful Windrider in honor of her uncanny ability to control the weather.

Ororo had already dedicated her life to helping people. But despite her godlike abilities, she never succumbed to the temptation to use her powers for personal gain.

My objective was to persuade Ororo to extend the scope of her powers, to help more than just a few tribes—to help all of humankind as a member of my X-Men. To my eternal gratitude, she agreed.

When Professor X came to Africa to ask me to join his X-Men, I knew little of evil. The people called me Beautiful Windrider, and I was as carefree as the breezes I caused to blow over that wild and radiant land. To me, evil was a drought that I had the power to vanquish, the power to bring sweet, life-giving rain to grateful people.

Now I have seen the evil people do to each other, and I can no more return to my innocence than I can go back to being a child. I am committed to the fight against wrongdoing wherever I find it. Yet I am haunted by the fear that while I fight the evil creeps inside me, like a night fog seeping under a closed door. Wasn't there a philosopher who once said, "If you stare into the abyss long enough, the abyss stares back at you"? If you fight evil long enough, must you become evil?

I asked myself that question many times down in the depths beneath New York City, in a place much like hell itself: the secret home of the mutant band known as Morlocks. Nightcrawler, Colossus, and I had come to that dreadful place to rescue our friend and fellow X-Man, Angel, from the clutches of Callisto, the Morlock Queen.

Ever since my childhood, when I was buried under rubble beside my dying mother, I have feared enclosed places. Though my conscious mind knew I was no longer a little girl separated forever from beloved parents by a plane crash, I nevertheless shuddered as I entered those inky depths.

The Morlocks' domain was actually quite extensive, but the darkness was as oppressive as a tomb. I was eager to save Angel, but instead of rescuing him, Colossus, Nightcrawler, and I walked right into Callisto's trap.

Experience has taught me never to judge character by appearance. Too many pure souls are trapped in misshapen bodies, or twisted souls in beautiful forms. In the case of our dear Professor X, a strong soul hides inside a crippled body, and in Beast's furry form lurks a supreme intellect.

But in Callisto's case I made an exception and I was not wrong. The first moment I saw her scarred face I feared the worst—and I was not disappointed! She wore a black patch over her missing right eye. A deep gouge ran down her forehead to her left cheek. Spiky black hair contrasted sharply with the unnaturally pale skin of an underground dweller. Her body had the wiry muscles of one who fights for the sheer animal joy of tearing flesh from bone.

Callisto had kidnapped Angel in the hopes of making him her consort. I sensed her motivation stemmed more from resentment of Angel's physical perfection than from real attraction, much less love for him. Callisto wanted to keep him, like a caged bird, in the nightmare realm where she ruled her band of outcast mutants.

Of course, we tried to escape. Colossus used his incredible strength to break the cords that bound us. Nightcrawler made a grab for Callisto, teleporting them both high above the reach of the renegade mutants.

And I summoned a storm inside the vast black tunnel to keep our enemy at bay. Lightning flashed, searing the darkness with brilliant spears, illuminating the shocked, misshapen faces of the assembled Morlocks. Thunder echoed off the arched stone walls.

We would have succeeded if Nightcrawler had killed Callisto right then. But, as he said, X-Men do not kill.

Instead, we tried to strike a deal for our freedom. Just then, a strange old woman took my hand.

"What harm can a little old lady do?" she cackled.

Then I felt a fever like fire in my veins. I heard the woman say her name was Plague, and then my head swam and I knew no more.

I woke, tied up once more, and heard Nightcrawler issue a challenge to Callisto.

Her taunt cleared the cobwebs from my clouded brain: "Sure you want to go through with it, chum? These duels are to the death."

I could not let Nightcrawler die in my place. Though I still felt ill from Plague's touch, I forced strength into my voice. "Callisto!" I shouted. "I lead the X-Men. The challenge, the duel, your life—are *mine!*"

Nightcrawler protested that I wasn't well enough to fight. But I was determined. I knew he could not do what was necessary. I loved him for that innocence, but innocence would not save our lives!

And I knew just what to say, since vanity is often evil's undoing. "I will fight—unless Callisto is afraid to face me."

True to form, the Morlock Queen accepted my challenge. I was forbidden to use my elemental powers. We would fight hand-to-hand, knife-to-knife—no holds barred!

Callisto had mutant strength, fierceness and cunning. But I was not the helpless fool she took me for! We circled each other, briefly assessing. I saw taut savagery eager for the kill. She saw only fever and weakness. Callisto's scarred face was twisted with cruel amusement. She was sure of her advantage: X-Men did not kill!

Callisto drew first blood, and that made her even more cocky. But the most basic rule of fighting is this: never underestimate your enemy. Callisto made that mistake. Luckily, she'd never been trained in Professor X's Danger Room!

In one sweeping move, I wrapped my cape around Callisto's arm and slashed. While she was still stunned by surprise and pain, I pulled her close and stabbed straight into her heart. I did not hesitate. I did not regret, even as Callisto collapsed to the floor.

Quickly, I freed Angel. Then, facing the astonished Morlocks, I declared, "By your laws, I now lead the Morlocks."

A sea of pale, uncertain faces stared back at me.

"There is no more need for you to hide. If you wish a home, a sanctuary, Professor Xavier will provide it, as he did for us," I offered.

The Morlock known as Caliban looked at me with huge yellow eyes. He shook his head. "Caliban knows your heart is true, Storm, and your word good. But this is where we belong."

I could not help thinking there might be wisdom in the strange mutant's words. Perhaps they could only thrive in darkness. But I was glad to hear Caliban's next words, "From this day forth, X-Men and Morlocks shall live in peace, as friends."

Nightcrawler's blue face expressed confusion. "Only minutes ago they sought our heads. Now, they let us pass without a murmur. How quickly and completely things change sometimes—and people, too."

I had no time for philosophy. I was eager to leave that dark domain. "Is Callisto alive?" I asked.

"Barely," he replied. "If not for the Morlocks' healer, she would be dead. Did you know you stabbed her through the heart?"

I heard the reproach in his voice.

"I knew what had to be done when I made the challenge," I told him, standing my ground.

Nightcrawler sounded sad. "I never expected that of you."

"Neither did Callisto," I replied. "That was her mistake."

And I would not have expected it of myself either, just a few years ago. But time changes all things, and people, too, just as it changes the weather. I am no longer Beautiful Windrider...I am Storm!

CHAPTER 8

Gambit

It is not surprising that a French term best describes the Cajun Gambit. *Joie de vivre* literally means "joy of life," which he possesses in abundance.

Fearless in battle, Gambit has the mutant ability to convert the potential energy stored in matter into kinetic energy. Any object, even one as small as the playing cards he habitually carries, can become a deadly weapon in his hands.

Around the mansion, Gambit has earned the nickname "Ragin' Cajun." Though I encourage all my X-Men to control their emotions, I cannot change their basic natures. Gambit is as fiery as his specialty, chicken Creole. Although he shares little about his shadowy past in the New Orleans Guild of Thieves, he clearly feels deep loyalty toward family and friends—and white-hot hatred for anyone who dares hurt the people he loves.

file: therapeutic debriefing
subfile: Remy LeBeau
codename: Gambit
password: chance

Sometimes de cards are good, and sometimes bad. Life is about playin' whatever hand you're dealt—and playin' to win! I carry cards to use as weapons and because I like dem—almost as much as I like de beautiful women. Y'see, *chère*, cards are like life. Luck, skill, de willingness to take risks: dese are what make a good gambler—and a good life, I guarantee!

But de Professor didn't ask me to talk philosophy into his fancy machine. Like de little child who can't fall asleep, he wants to hear a story. Well, I tell a story about luck and chance.

It started one night in de Danger Room at de Professor's school here in Salem Center. You never know what's goin' to happen in de Danger Room, which is why I like it! De computer creates enemies, settings, and weapons as varied as possible poker hands—and as real as de rain dat soaks de bayou.

Dat night, I was takin' my chances with a sweet little lady called Rogue. We'd been fendin' off everythin' de room could dish out: bullets, lasers, Sentinels. I was having fun, but Rogue, she was so serious.

"Smile, *chère!*" I said. "Enjoy the game."

Rogue's dazzlin' green eyes flashed. "Gambit! This is no game!" she scolded, just as missiles burst from de Danger Room walls.

Even as I dodged de dangerous explosives, I laughed to myself. "Life is a game!" I told Rogue. "I'll show you."

She shouted to warn me against another volley of missiles headin' straight for my back.

"Gambit!" she repeated.

I stood my ground, as if I didn't hear.

"Remy!" Rogue screamed my real name, the one only close friends and family use. My lips twitched with a secret smile. I love a passionate woman! I only hoped dat Storm and Wolverine, who were behind de Danger Room's control panel, would have de good sense not to end de game before my ace was played.

Rogue smashed into me with all de force her beautiful body could muster. De blow knocked me to safety as de missiles rocked de room with dere deafenin' blast.

We lay face to face in a tangle of arms and

legs. For a moment I gazed into her lovely green eyes, savorin' our impromptu embrace.

"Now isn't dis a cozy *tête-à-tête, chère?*" I asked as the program ended and the room reverted to its normal configuration.

Rogue's heart pounded against mine, relief, fear, and passion mixin' in its frantic beat. Den my keen senses detected somethin' more, somethin' outside de Danger Room, but within de security boundaries of de mansion compound. "Love to stay here all day, but we've got company," I said, leaping up to investigate.

The intruder was very sneaky. I barely detected his breathin', de feather-whisper of his feet on de mansion's floor. But I was sneakier. Before you could say "shrimp gumbo," I had pressed a card to our visitor's throat, ready to charge it with a fatal dose of energy.

Den a familiar voice, with a Cajun accent even thicker dan mine, said, "Put dat card away, Remy! You still a thief, I hope...not an assassin."

It was my dear brother, Henri! It had been too long since de last time I saw him.

By then, de other X-Men in residence had joined us. Wolverine was as cranky as an old gator wonderin' how Henri got past the

mansion's security system. But I didn't want to waste time explainin' de secrets of our guild. Does a magician tell you how he gets de rabbit out of de hat? Besides, I couldn't wait to hear de news from de Big Easy, New Orleans.

De news, I'm afraid, was not good. On the porch overlooking the mansion's garden, Henri explained dat de peace between de Guild of Assassins and de Guild of Thieves had been broken. My family, de Thieves, was in trouble.

"Come home, Remy. Ain't nothin' more important den family!" Henri said.

Den out of nowhere, dis arrow whooshes through the air and into his chest!

Henri! My dear brother! As the lifeblood oozed out of him, he begged me to go home, to find out why de Assassins were killing de Thieves. Den he asked me to bring him to rest beside our father.

"Yes...brother," I swore, though I knew Henri could no longer hear me. The red-stained chest was as still as a stone.

My blood boiled with rage. Dere were only two ways dis game could end: Whoever had dared to rob my brother of his life would either die by my hand—or kill me, too!

Rogue, Wolverine, and Storm raced to my side. Wolverine sniffed de air. "I got their scent," he growled. "Two of 'em headed toward Salem Center. We can catch them easy."

But it wasn't easy at all. De killers led us all the way down to New Orleans. De danger we faced was far worse than de Guild of Assassins. Dey had only been killing Thieves because dey were under de influence of de Brood—egg-laying aliens who take over de bodies of dere hosts.

Dis we learned from de Ghost Rider. Now he is a story all to himself, but I'll tell you dis much. Danny Ketch is an ordinary teenager until innocent blood is spilled; den he becomes an avenging spirit. De power comes to him from de strange motorcycle he found on de night of his sister's death.

I reckon plenty of innocent blood had been spilled by dat ugly Brood Queen. And dat's how Rogue, Wolverine, Beast, Cyclops, Jubilee, and I came to be in a tunnel deep under de French Quarter with a biker whose head was a flaming skull—tracking de monster dat killed my brother!

Ghost Rider looked down de dark tunnel and said, "The Brood Queen's lair is ahead. The time for vengeance is upon us."

"De Queen is mine!" I said.

"Save a piece for me," Wolverine added.

Ever the leader, Cyclops said, "Let's not forget our main objective, gentlemen!"

"De children!" I'd been so bent on revenge I'd almost forgotten dat de Brood Queen had captured de children of both de Thieves and Assassins Guilds. We had to rescue dem before the foul creature changed dem into broodlings.

Wolverine's nose led us down a steep, dark tunnel dripping with stalactites. De tunnel opened onto a vast underground chamber.

"We're on the Brood's ground. The attack can come from anywhere!" Cyclops warned.

We advanced in a tight formation, eyes straining in de shadows. Den by de light of Ghost Rider's flaming skull, we saw...de horror!

De children were alive, but cocooned in a sticky mass of fibers, like flies in a spider's web. Dere panicked faces peered out of de goo. "Help us, please!" one begged.

"Just hold on, little darlin'." Wolverine's adamantium claws snicked out of his hands. "We'll have you out of there in no time."

"Be gentle but quick!" Cyclops urged. "These

kids have been through enough. They don't need to be in the middle of a Brood attack. I'll keep watch."

And dat's when I noticed dat Ghost Rider had slipped away from de group. "Speaking of watch," I said, "where are you going, *mon ami?*"

"The path of vengeance leads to the Brood Queen." He stalked off. I ran after him, determined dat vengeance would be mine!

Wolverine caught our scent—and de Brood Queen's—and followed us while de others took care of de children. De uncanny light of Ghost Rider's skull flickered on de tunnel's cold walls. Wolverine sniffed de damp air.

"Company!" he announced. "Lots of it."

I pulled a card from my deck and saw his metal claws flash. Yet I saw no enemy. "What are dey waitin' for? I can hear dem breathin'..."

Suddenly dey sprang from every corner. I flung card after blazing card into a hissing, tentacled mass of...the Brood!

"Dis feels good!" With each blow I imagined breaking de arrow that killed my brother. "But where is de Queen?" I demanded. We were up to our ankles in alien blood. Wolverine sniffed de air. "She's here!"

I suddenly realized de wall I was standing beside was not a wall at all, but de enormous body of the Brood Queen! Her long teeth gleamed in the flaming light cast by Ghost Rider's head. She was some ugly! Whoo-eee! Her voice echoed off the walls, "I have watched you slaughter my children, mammals, and for that I will have my vengeance. Your deaths will come after you witness the slaughter of *your* children."

Her spidery legs carried her vast bulk nimbly up the tunnel. Ghost Rider, Wolverine, and I raced after her.

Ghost Rider's magical motorcycle appeared beside him, and he roared after de Queen, leaving a blazing trail of flame in his wake. I could only watch with jealousy as Ghost Rider flung a heavy chain around de Queen's neck and dragged her up to de street. By the time I caught up with him, Ghost Rider had already brought de Brood Queen down.

"Let's make sure." Wolverine plunged his claws into de monster's enormous, red eye.

"Done!" I flung a card to sever her head. Then I shook Ghost Rider's bony hand. "I owe you a debt of honor, *mon ami!*"

As he roared off on his motorcycle, I realized I had another debt to pay—to my brother. I saw Henri buried beside our father. Den I danced to dat Cajun zydeco music with de prettiest woman I could fin'. Den I danced with her sister, and stole a kiss or two. Den I cooked up a batch of my best chicken Creole and had myself a big ol' party—just de way Henri would've wanted it. Because life is a gamble. Sometimes you win and sometimes you lose. But the point is to keep playin' your best until de game is over, I guarantee!

CHAPTER 9

Jubilee

Jubilation Lee is the youngest member of the current X-Men. Once a high school dropout, Jubilee now excels in her studies at my institute, the Xavier School for Gifted Youngsters. Although she tends to be a bit flighty, a common flaw of youth, Jubilee's determination to become a full-fledged member of the X-Men has given her a great motivation to succeed.

My toughest task as Jubilee's mentor has been to hold her back from dangerous missions, for which I believe she is not yet ready. Within the school's supportive atmosphere, Jubilee is learning to control her mutant abilities and recovering from the recent tragic death of her foster parents.

Jubilee's powers allow her to emit and control energy *plasmoids* varying in shape from spheres to streamers, and in intensity from dazzling fireworks to deadly explosives. I, for one, am glad this young dynamo is on our side!

file: therapeutic debriefing
subfile: Jubilation Lee
codename: Jubilee
password: compassion

When I found out my parents had been murdered and that these two thugs named Remo and Molokai had done it, you can bet I was bent on revenge! But they were in Los Angeles, and that meant I had to get back there, which was a bit of a problem. Wolverine and I were stuck in the Australian outback in this stainless steel Ant Hill that was a major hangout for Sentinels, these big purple robots who hate mutants. Well, this batch of Sentinels even hated "normal" people.

Now, you might ask, *how can a robot hate anything?* Well the thing is, most Sentinels don't. They were just programmed by this weird scientist who was convinced mutants were a threat to mankind. So their programming told them to find and stomp all mutants.

But the Sentinels in the Ant Hill were different. Their leader had actually started thinking on his own. Professor X uses some special word to describe it—*sentient*, I think—but all I know is, this robot started having his own ideas. Like, *how about building this big machine that will cause a solar flare that would turn all humans crispier than chili fries?*

On a really bad hair day I might think something like that, just for a second. But this Sentinel actually went ahead and built this huge planet-toasting widget. And Wolverine and I were the only ones around who could stop him! (Talk about pressure! This was like finals times a thousand!)

It's hard to describe the Ant Hill because it's not like any place a human would build. The walls are all metal and everywhere you look there are giant machines. I felt like a sardine in a really big can. I couldn't wait to get out and see the sunshine—but not the kind of sunshine those Sentinels had in mind!

Wolverine and I were surrounded by five of those gnarly purple robots and I've gotta tell you, those guys are big! We barely came up to their ankles. But Wolverine's not scared of anything, so he just dove into one of them—claws first!

Talk about nails to die for! Wolverine sliced that Sentinel right in two. The others blasted at us, but wound up hitting the top half of their buddy as it smashed to the ground. Pretty funny, huh? But I was too busy running to laugh.

"Bob and weave!" Wolverine yelled to me. "Don't give their trackin' computers a pattern to get a bead on."

So I was dodging this way and that, with megablasts from the Sentinels' weird red eyes exploding all around me.

"Have you got a plan or are we just running for our lives?" I screamed over the blasts.

I was hoping Wolverine would say, "It's a great plan that can't fail, kid. We'll destroy the solar-flare generator and get back to L.A. in time for lunch." But instead, he had just a bit of a plan, and I could tell he wasn't exactly sure it would work.

Meanwhile, we were running down more creepy metal halls, like rats in a maze—and guess what? We hit a dead end!

I felt this rush of panic and anger, so I snapped at Wolvie, "I hope this plan of yours is totally wizard. Because I do *not* intend to end up as a smear on the bottom of a big purple foot! Not now that I know who killed my parents! I'm going to find Remo and Molokai and..."

Wolverine slapped his hand over my mouth and said, "Cool it, Jubilee! You gotta channel that anger if you wanna make it back to L.A. for your payback. You gotta get your act together and help me throw down heavy on the big purple guys!"

Then we heard the clang clang of huge metal feet on metal floors, and my heart started pounding like it was fighting its way out of my chest.

"Here's where we open a six pack o' trouble and shove it in their face!" Wolverine said. (Isn't he the cutest?) I heard the claws snick out of his hands as Wolverine shouted to me, "Go for his memory banks!"

So I paffed this Sentinel's head for all I was worth! (Paffing is what I call it when I use my powers, 'cause of the sound it makes.) Then I saw Wolverine get slapped against the metal wall and for one horrible second, I thought I was going to be stuck in that dreadful place all alone.

But Wolverine's tough. "I'm coming back on the rebound, darlin'," he called. "You hit the other Sentinel's vision receptors."

Paf! I felt like two lightning bolts were streaming out of my hands! And the *zap* when the bolts hit their mark was incredible. So I wasn't exactly surprised to hear this robotic voice drone, "Optic sensors disabled."

Which gave Wolverine a chance to slice the head off that robot.

"Paf it, Jubilee!" he yelled.

But the head landed in the other Sentinel's arms. And he said, "No. This unit will protect you, 86."

My jaw dropped open. I mean, who ever heard of a robot caring for its buddy? Like, who ever heard of a robot even having a buddy? This was weird!

Then the surviving Sentinel just kind of lost it. Light came pouring out of him like fireworks on the Fourth of July. I guess all his circuits blew out from the strain of trying to save his friend.

The whole floor shook when the Sentinel fell over, which makes sense when you realize one of those things is as tall as a building. Anyway, I found myself staring into its glowing red eyes. And it said, "Don't turn this unit off... This unit is...apprehensive of the...darkness."

This was major heavy. I mean, I knew it was just a machine and all, but I couldn't kill it! I ran into Wolverine's arms, buried my face against his hairy chest and just sort of shuddered because this machine was afraid to die—just like me! (Life can be scary, you know?)

Then the main Sentinel showed up, the one with the crazy plan to fry all humanity. So the gloves were off. I mean, this giant toaster was about to get burnt!

Wolvie turned to me. "I'll rip, and you paf!"

But before we could fly into action, the Sentinel held up one of his huge hands. I don't know how he did it, but he set up this time/stasis field to slow us down while he "processed new data," trying to "understand" why one Sentinel would die trying to save another, and why I couldn't bring myself to kill him. Anyway, Wolvie and I tried to move, but it was like swimming through cold peanut butter. Gross!

Finally, the big purple robot dude terminated the stasis field and asked us to explain feelings like compassion and empathy and caring. Which really ticked me off. I mean, any second now he's going to barbecue us all and he wants to *chat?* So I said, "What about the whole world full of people who are gonna get extra crispy real soon?"

Well, guess what? The Sentinel changed his mind. I guess that means he really has one! He said, "There will be no solar flare. There will be no mass incineration." And he even destroyed the solar flare generator gadget and erased the plans for how it was built.

Then he said he was going to spend the next two thousand years or so rewriting the Sentinels' software to include human emotions. And with a *whoosh*, he sent me and Wolvie right back to Los Angeles, which was a really neat trick and a big savings on air fare!

There was no time for thinking "Wow, we saved the world." Because I was too bent on getting the scum that killed my folks. So the next day, Wolvie and I went to this sleazy office in Hollywood where Remo and Molokai's boss worked. And in his usual polite manner, Wolvie "persuaded" the jerk to tell us where his thugs were (or else!).

By the time we found 'em it was dark. They were on a quiet street just outside of L.A., beatin' up some poor loser for their boss. We "borrowed" their car and drove up this big, lonely hill, so there wouldn't be any witnesses or bystanders to get hurt.

When they caught up to us at the top of the hill, I paffed the guns right out of their hands, which really surprised them! I paffed their eyes for good measure. And while they were stumbling around trying to figure out what hit 'em, I kicked the big guy—Molokai—right in the gut. The other one got it in the kisser.

Wolvie said, "Looks like you got these two ol' boys where you want 'em, Jubilee."

I stood over them, energy crackling in my fists, knowing I could kill them with one paf. It was like Wolvie was reading my mind, because he said, "It don't take much, darlin'. Just a very accurate paf right in the cerebral cortex. Not even traceable. Just an odd coincidence—two healthy thugs havin' strokes at the same time."

I couldn't tell whether he was trying to tempt me or what.

"Would feel good, wouldn't it? If you were that kind of person, that is," Wolvie continued, his voice level and quiet.

"You've killed plenty of people," I said.

Wolverine tossed his cigar away. "Yeah. Wanna sit up with me one night and talk to them all?"

Then I knew for sure what he was doing. Wolvie was trying to tell me that killing's not worth it. Killing Remo and Molokai wouldn't

bring back my parents. All it would do is give me this dark spot in my heart—and who needs that?

I saw the lights of Los Angeles twinkling in the valley below us. And I saw Wolverine's face. And I suddenly had this feeling that, like, it's a beautiful world, despite all the bad things that happen. And I don't want to add to its darkness.

But, of course, I was still mad. So I kicked them both again for good measure. Then I turned away and said, "I guess I'm just weak, huh?"

It felt good to have Wolverine walking beside me. He smiled and said, "No, darlin', that ain't weakness. You got enough heart to save the world...and as a matter o' fact, you did."

Not bad, huh? I guess I've earned a trip to the mall!

If you liked this book, here's a taste of...

Wolverine: Top Secret

There's only a window between us now. I break through it.

"You're...you're...*dead!*" the Professor stutters.

I grab him tightly. "Am I...dead?" I say. "Is...that what...you've...done to me?...Made me a walking...*dead man?*"

"You're an animal," the Professor spits out. "A trained animal."

"*I...am...Logan!*" I say. "I...am...a man. You ...are the...animal!"

BOOKS IN THIS SERIES